The Little Frog That Wasn't

By Jody Perkins

There was a lily pad in a beautiful pond, right at the bottom of a very tall mountain.

Sitting on this lily pad was Esofel, a very special frog. You see, this frog wasn't green!

He was a beautiful, beautiful blue.

He wasn't too dark blue

and he wasn't too light,

but just a very special "just right blue".

He wasn't a fat frog either; he was a slim and sleek frog.

Now some of the other frogs made fun of Esofel because he wasn't like all the rest of the frogs in the pond. Sometimes this made Esofel very sad.

So one day when he was feeling really, really, sad, his mother told him that she would make a very special coat for him out of lush green moss. Which she did.

When the coat was finished Esofel put it on and went to sit on his lily pad. How very proud he was.

Now the other frogs thought he was very lucky to have such a beautiful coat. His best friend Taba asked if he could borrow the coat one day. Being a very kind frog, Esofel wasn't afraid to say yes, you may borrow my special coat.

Taba only had the coat for a very few minutes, but he was not as careful as he should have been. In fact, he fell "ker plop" right into a mud puddle.

He was really upset with himself, so he took the coat right home to his Mother to wash it. But alas, the coat was ruined because it had shrunk two sizes.

Taba felt really awful about this, but he had to take the coat back to Esofel. Now Esofel was not mad, but he did feel bad because he loved his green coat as it really made him feel like all the other frogs.

Esofel had another friend; in fact this was a very, very, special friend. She was a lovely yellow butterfly and her name was Sparkle

Sometimes she would land right on Esofel's head and that would make him laugh. More often, she would sit on a rock nearby the lily pad.

Sparkle told Esofel that he should be proud that he was blue. Because he wasn't like all the rest of the frogs, he was special and she loved him just the way he was.

Early in the mornings Esofel and Sparkle would jump and fly about and have a grand time. Of course it was Sparkle who flew and Esofel that jumped.

They would sometimes meet Taba and all three would play together. At lunch time all three would look for bugs...

They each would catch a few and then share with each other.

After lunch, the two frogs would sun themselves on a lily pad and the butterfly on her rock. After all, they had a busy morning.....

About the Author

Jody was born and raised in Amesbury, Massachusetts. Her given name was Joanne, but when she was in Junior High School, her friends decided to call her Jody – and it stuck.

Many years ago she took a course in Children's Literature at a local college. She wrote a few children's stories, but shortly after, tragedy struck her family and she had to stop writing.

Now many years later, she is "back on track" and hoping her stories will make children happy.

About the Illustrator

David Shaw's career was in education for many years, serving as an elementary teacher and on up to principal of two schools. In the art field he has illustrated a manual for a speech prosthesis called Mr. Big Mouth. He has done a number of coloring books including one on Fire Safety for elementary school training. He did a calendar of historical buildings for his town and has a series of note cards that includes those illustrations among other things. He has also illustrated eight poetry books and four children's books.

Other Stories by Jody Perkins

Fluffy

This is a children's story of a bunny with a very fluffy tail that gets in trouble along with his brother and sister for eating carrots from the neighbor's garden.

The Little Green Man

This is a children's story of a lonely green man who befriends

a cat with green eyes and a beautiful green parakeet.

Made in the USA
Middletown, DE
30 November 2016